PUFFIN BOOKS

NO PRIZE OR PRESENTS FOR SAM

Sam is having a wonderful time in the country with his cousin Ginger until he finds out about the Most Unusual Pets Competition to be held at the village fête. The trouble is that although he's always wanted a pet, he can't have one because normally he lives in a flat in town, where animals are not allowed. But Sam is determined to enter the competition and sets out to find himself a pet ... and his choice has some unexpected repercussions!

Christmas is coming and Sam is getting really excited thinking about the presents he will get from Father Christmas. But then disaster strikes, and his Aunty loses her job. It looks as if Christmas will be a very poor affair this year and there'll be no presents. Then Sam decides he must do something to help and is determined to find himself a job and earn enough money to give his Aunty and Uncle a happy Christmas. But it's very difficult for an eight-year-old to find something to do which will earn him some money.

These two stories about Sam's determination will entertain and amuse young readers.

Thelma Lambert is an artist and designer who lives in London with her husband and family. She has also written and illustrated *The Disappearing Cat*, which includes another story about Sam and is published in Puffin.

GW00808689

Another book by Thelma Lambert

THE DISAPPEARING CAT

NO PRIZE
OR PRESENTS
FOR SAM

written and illustrated by
THELMA LAMBERT

PUFFIN BOOKS

PUFFIN BOOKS

Published by the Penguin Group
27 Wrights Lane, London w8 5tz, England
Viking Penguin Inc., 40 West 23rd Street, New York, New York 10010, USA
Penguin Books Australia Ltd, Ringwood, Victoria, Australia
Penguin Books Canada Ltd, 2801 John Street, Markham, Ontario, Canada l3r 1b4
Penguin Books (NZ) Ltd, 182–190 Wairau Road, Auckland 10, New Zealand

Penguin Books Ltd, Registered Offices: Harmondsworth, Middlesex, England

No Prize for Sam first published by Hamish Hamilton Children's Books, 1986
No Presents for Sam first published by Hamish Hamilton Children's Books, 1987
Published in Puffin Books in one volume 1988
1 3 5 7 9 10 8 6 4 2

Text and illustrations copyright © Thelma Lambert, 1986, 1987
All rights reserved

Made and printed in Great Britain by
Richard Clay Ltd, Bungay, Suffolk
Filmset in Baskerville

Except in the United States of America,
this book is sold subject to the condition
that it shall not, by way of trade or otherwise,
be lent, re-sold, hired out, or otherwise circulated
without the publisher's prior consent in any form of
binding or cover other than that in which it is
published and without a similar condition
including this condition being imposed
on the subsequent purchaser

Contents

NO PRIZE FOR SAM

For my brother,
Peter Lambert

Chapter One

Sam was looking forward to staying in the country because he thought he'd see plenty of animals there. Sam lived in a town flat where animals were not allowed. But he always longed for a real pet of his own.

And now Sam was going to the country to stay with his cousin

Ginger. Ginger was a friendly boy of eleven. Sam was tall, and looked the same age as his cousin, but Sam was only eight. Sam was also a little accident-prone. The first day of the holiday Ginger took Sam to see all his best things — the hollow tree, the owl's nest, Ferdinand the bull. When they came home for tea, Ginger's Mum gave a great shriek — "SAM! What *have* you been doing?"

Sam *was* a sight: his trousers were covered in mud, his shirt was torn, and his face was scratched.

"Sam got his head stuck in the hollow tree," explained Ginger. "Then he fell in a cow-pat running away from Ferdy, then he tore his shirt on a fence . . ."

Sam just grinned. He'd enjoyed every minute.

Next day the two boys passed a poster outside the village shop. LEMSFORD SUMMER FETE, it said. AUGUST 26th. TO BE HELD IN THE VICARAGE GARDEN. FLOWER AND VEGETABLE SHOW. DONKEY RIDES. CREAM TEAS. RUNNING RACES AND COMPETITIONS. BABY SHOW .

4

Then right down at the bottom of the poster —

CHILDREN'S SPECIAL COMPETITION FOR THE MOST UNUSUAL PET.

"Gosh! I wish I had a pet for that competition," sighed Sam.

"You could go half shares in my pet rat," offered Ginger.

Sam thanked him but he said it wasn't the same.

All the children in the village were entering their pets: Sophie Cox had a tortoise; Johnny Bates-Next-Door his rabbit with one brown ear and one white; Jill Maskell her parrot; and Nigel Bodham was, he said, entering a . . . MONKEY! He told everyone that his father was buying him the monkey from Munts' Pet Shop in Lemmington.

When Sam heard about Munts he got very excited. "Let's go and see if they have a pet I could buy," he said.

So Sam and Ginger cycled to Lemmington and pressed their noses to Munts' window. There was the monkey wearing a little red jacket; it was £35. They went inside. They looked at rabbits, budgies, guinea-pigs ... Sam only had 50p and it wasn't enough to buy even a goldfish.

As they cycled home they passed a blackboard propped up against a gate. LIVE HENS FOR SALE ONLY 50p was scrawled in chalk.

"Hey! Did you see that?" said Ginger. "It's Scroggins' battery farm."

"What's a battery farm?" asked Sam.

"They keep the hens in cages and all the eggs come out on a long conveyor belt — "

"Just like a factory!" said Sam. "Not much fun for the hens, poor things . . ."

Scroggins' Farm consisted of several black huts. Mr Scroggins, clutching a whisky bottle, lurched round the corner of one of the huts.

8

"Excuse me, but we'd like to buy a chicken," said Ginger boldly.

"A shicken," he hiccupped. "Tha's fifty pensh . . . "

He staggered off to his office.

"Quick! Let's have a look at the batteries!" said Sam.

9

A door stood ajar and the boys peeped in. There were rows of tiny cages each with a chicken inside. They looked the most miserable creatures on earth. The whole place smelt as if it hadn't been cleaned for years. The boys came out, feeling a bit sick, and Sam was near to tears.

Mr Scroggins handed over a bulging plastic bag, and Sam paid him with his 50p piece.

"At last I've got a pet of my very own," smiled Sam.

"Why are they so cheap, Mr Scroggins?" asked Ginger.

"Well, they've stopped laying eggs, see, and just fit for the pot . . . Still, you've got a bargain there, boy!" he said as he stumbled away.

Sam opened the bag and a scraggy head poked out. "I'll call you Belinda," he said. "Because you look a bit like my old Granny Belinda."

Chapter Two

When they got home they took Belinda to Ginger's garden shed. The chicken couldn't even stand up, but just lay there, helplessly. She had hardly any feathers, and red skin showed through. She looked at death's door.

"I don't think she'll last the night," said Ginger gloomily.

Sam was so worried he decided to tuck Belinda up in his own bed. When his aunt saw, she said, "Get that horrible looking hen out of here *at once*!"

Poor Sam had to spend the next hour helping his aunt wash his sheets, as Belinda had made a terrible mess of them.

But in the morning Belinda was not only alive, but walking about the shed. Ginger bought a bag of chicken feed and they gave some to Belinda. She didn't even know how to peck — she had been used to factory food. But she soon learned.

"We must make her a home of her own," said Sam. They made her a

little house out of an old cupboard.
The drawer made a good nesting-box,
lined with grass. Sam filled a bowl
with water, and Belinda's new home
was ready. Tenderly Sam put her
inside where she cowered in a corner.

"When we've made a garden for
her we can let her out in the open,"
said Sam.

That afternoon the boys went on an errand for Ginger's mum to earn a few pence. As Sam said, they would need money to buy food for Belinda: the chicken feed cost 80p a bag.

On the way home for tea, Sam suddenly stopped.

"Look! There's someone up that tree! What's he doing?"

There was a man, half way up a big oak tree. "Are you all right?" called Ginger.

"I'm fine, thanks . . . " There was a silence, followed by a crashing of branches, and a jolly looking man landed beside them in a shower of leaves.

"Oh!" he panted, "I hope that one comes out all right! A beautiful

16

specimen — the best green wood-pecker I've ever seen!" He smiled broadly. "By the way, my name's Tom Purvis and I photograph birds!"

He explained he was a reporter from the local paper, and he was doing a feature of all the unusual birds in the district.

"Do you boys know of any unusual birds around here?"

"Oh yes, we do," they said.

Ginger and Sam took Tom Purvis to see the owl in the old barn.

Sam rushed forward eagerly to have a better look and fell head first into the water butt with a mighty SPLASH! The owl flapped off.

"Oh how beautiful! I've never seen
an owl flying before!" spluttered Sam.

"Yes," said the photographer
trying to smile. "It is beautiful, but
I've missed the picture now . . ."

"I've got an unusual bird," said Sam.

Ginger was embarrassed and gave Sam a sharp nudge. He didn't think Mr Purvis would be interested in an old battery hen that could hardly stand up. But Sam was persistent.

"It's all red coloured and it's got hardly any feathers," he said.

"What kind of a bird is it?" asked Tom curiously.

"It's a factory bird called Belinda," said Sam.

Tom Purvis laughed. "All right. I think I'd like to see your Belinda!"

Sam led the reporter home, dripping water all along the lane.

When Tom saw Belinda, he was very shocked. "Where did you get this chicken?" he said.

"I bought her at Scroggins' Farm,"
said Sam. "I'm entering her for the
Unusual Pet Competition at the
Fête."

"She's certainly unusual," said Tom Purvis grimly. "I've never seen a chicken like that before."

And he took a photograph of poor, battered Belinda.

Chapter Three

Sam and Ginger made a little garden
for Belinda. Then they persuaded her
to come out. She looked suspiciously
at the green stuff under her feet.

"She's never seen grass before!"
cried Sam.

"Or felt the rain," said Ginger. "Or
the sun — she doesn't know about

night and day. They keep the lights on all the time in battery farms to make them lay more eggs . . . "

Day by day Belinda got stronger. Her feathers began to grow, her eyes became bright. She no longer cowered in fright when they came near, but rushed to greet whoever came to feed her.

Meanwhile there was the problem of paying for Belinda's bags of chicken feed. They earned money by doing odd jobs, and soon every window in the village gleamed brightly.

Then came the great day when Sam found an egg in the nesting box.

Ginger's Mum was washing the

kitchen floor when Sam came running in holding the small brown egg.

"LOOK!" he cried. "BELINDA'S LAID AN EGG!"

"Watch out!" shouted his aunt. But too late. Sam was flat on his face and the egg was splattered all over the newly cleaned floor.

"Oh, SAM!" sighed his aunt. "What a mess!"

But after that there was an egg every morning in the nesting-box.

"I'm sorry I ever called Belinda a horrible hen!" smiled Ginger's Mum. "She's a little treasure now!"

Chapter Four

It was a perfect summer's day for the Fête. Ginger and Sam arrived early to help the vicar put out the deck-chairs on the lawn. But Sam was more trouble than he was worth since he managed to trap his fingers in a deck-chair and had to be taken to the First Aid Tent for a bandage . . .

Soon people were arriving thick and fast, and the band struck up a rousing tune. The donkey began his stint up and down the drive, and the races and competitions began. The Unusual Pet Competition was the last of the afternoon.

Everyone seemed to be winning something: Sophie Cox's baby sister

won the baby show; Mr Bates-Next-Door won a First Prize for his marrow and Ginger's Mum a Second for her plum jam.

At last the Unusual Pet Competition was announced.

Ginger had entered his black-tailed rat, and then there was Sophie Cox and her tortoise, Johnnie Bates' rabbit with the odd ears, Jill's parrot and many more. Andy Tonks had dressed his dog in a Boy Scouts uniform, and at the end of the line was Nigel Bodham and his monkey.

A large lady in pink, Mrs Digby-Smith, was the judge. She wore a big hat trimmed with roses. She came down the line of children, the flowers on her hat bobbing as she bent to

speak to each one. When she came to
Sam she patted Belinda on the head.

"Lovely chicken, dear," she
murmured. She probably thought
that Sam had just borrowed a hen
from the family hen-house for the
afternoon . . .

She admired the tortoise, the rabbit, the parrot —

Everyone was looking at the little table with the prizes on — who would win this, the last competition of the day?

Ginger won Third Prize for his

black-tailed rat (a box of fudge). The dog dressed as a Boy Scout came Second. He won an electric torch.

"Now for the First Prize!" cried Mrs Digby-Smith. And she handed Nigel Bodham the magnificent set of binoculars.

"I just had to choose this adorable monkey! He's the most — "

But Mrs Digby-Smith never finished her sentence because at that moment the monkey leaned over and pulled Belinda's tail. Sam, furious, smacked the monkey smartly on the head. The monkey snatched Mrs Digby-Smith's beautiful hat, put it on its own head, and with a terrific leap disappeared in the direction of the tea-tent. The competition ended in

uproar as the dog dressed as a Boy
Scout gave chase to the monkey, and
Belinda set up a loud cackling.

The monkey tore through the tea-tent leaving a trail of destruction: he ran over the 'Guess the Weight' cake leaving little footprints in the icing; he threw biscuits around, had a fight with the Boy Scout and ended up by biting the vicar's wife in the ankle . . .

"That monkey's a dangerous animal; that Bodham boy doesn't know how to look after it," said Tom Purvis, the photographer. "Hello, Ginger, hello Sam!" smiled Tom. "And how did you do in the pet competition?"

Ginger told him about winning Third Prize.

"And what about Sam? No prize for Sam?" said Tom, pulling a long face.

"I didn't get a prize," said Sam. "Here's my pet. Remember that chicken you took a picture of? Well, I looked after her until she was well again . . . "

Proudly, Sam lifted Belinda out of her basket for Tom to see.

He stared in amazement at the hen, her brown feathers gleaming, her eyes bright. "That's never the same chicken?" Tom couldn't believe his eyes. "Why — she's beautiful!"

"She lays an egg every day now," said Sam. "And Mr Scroggins said

36

she'd stopped laying! Said she was only fit for the pot — "

"I'd like to take some photos of Belinda," said Tom suddenly.

And he took several pictures of Sam, proudly holding his Unusual Pet.

Just then Nigel appeared, having retrieved his monkey. "I say, don't you want a picture of me any my monkey? We did win First Prize, you know!"

"Ah, well, I seem to have used up all my film . . . " said Tom, winking at Ginger and Sam.

37

Ginger's Mum breathed a small sigh of relief: it was the last day of Sam's visit.

A tearful goodbye had just been said to Belinda, when Mr Bates-Next-Door called out over the fence,

"Have you seen this week's *Lemmington Gazette*? You're on the front page, Sam, you and your Belinda!"

They all crowded round to look at the paper.

Sure enough on the front page were two photographs: one showed Belinda as she had been six weeks ago, featherless and hardly able to stand up. And the other was of her at the Fête, looking the picture of health.

SCANDAL OF SCROGGINS' FARM ran the headline.

Ginger's Dad started to read.

"Good heavens!" he said. "They've called in the R.S.P.C.A. It seems Scroggins' Farm might be closed down . . . they found the place in a disgraceful state . . . "

"I always thought they'd have to do something about that farm one day," said Ginger's Mum. "Everyone knows old Scroggins is always drunk."

39

Ginger started to read out: " 'The plight of the chickens at this farm was brought to light by eight year old Sam Davis, who bought a hen from Scroggins'. This hen was barely alive. Thanks to Sam's loving care the hen became a healthy bird, as our pictures show. The *Lemmington Gazette* has reported the matter to the authorities concerned.' Gosh!" breathed Ginger.

"You're famous now, Sam!"

Ginger's Mum gave Sam a big hug. "You may not have won a prize, Sam, but you've won something much more important!"

And Sam understood what his aunt meant.

NO PRESENTS FOR SAM

Chapter One

Sam hurried down the High Street to look in the toy shop window. Yes, it was still there, the wonderful castle with battlements and towers. Sam pressed his nose hard against the window. How he would love a castle like that! What hours of fun he could have with his soldiers storming those battlements . . .

Sam lived in a small flat with his Uncle Dennis and his Aunty Kathleen. They were older than his friends' mums and dads; Uncle Dennis was retired and Aunty Kathleen worked as a dinner-lady at a school. So Sam knew that expensive things like big wooden castles were not to be thought of . . . But he couldn't help hoping.

Especially now, as it was nearly

December, because that meant that
Christmas was coming. Perhaps he
could write to Father Christmas
about the castle? But Sam was too old
to believe in Father Christmas! And
he wouldn't even tell his Aunt and
Uncle about wanting it, for Sam knew
that all their money was needed to
pay for things like food and gas bills.

It began to get dark and Sam set off
for home. The lit-up windows of the

High Street looked exciting just now, for the shops were all decorated for Christmas. They gave Sam a warm, happy feeling inside as he walked past. It was freezing cold, and he thought longingly of supper. Sam began to hurry home.

But when Sam got home, there was no smell of supper cooking, and he knew at once that there was something wrong. His happy feeling disappeared and Sam suddenly turned all cold inside.

His Aunty Kathleen had been crying.

Uncle Dennis put his arm around Sam.

"Your Aunt's a bit upset," he said. "She's just lost her job. You see, they don't need so many dinner-ladies now . . ."

Aunty Kathleen blew her nose.

"Don't look so worried, Sam!" she said. "I'll get another job soon. But I'm afraid it'll mean a rather frugal Christmas."

"What's frugal mean, Aunty?" said Sam.

"It means being careful with money. Not being able to buy things." His Aunt sighed. "I'm afraid there'll be no Christmas presents this year, Sam . . . "

That night in bed Sam couldn't go to sleep. He kept thinking of his Aunt's tear-stained face. He decided that, somehow or other, he would earn some money. He'd make his Aunt and

Uncle proud of him. He'd buy them food, get Aunty Kathleen that blue cardigan he knew she wanted ... Sam was determined to start work the very next day.

Chapter Two

But if you are only eight, there aren't many things you can do to earn money.

He was too young to deliver papers, or baby-sit, or anything much. After a week Sam earned fifty pence by doing odd jobs for neighbours, running errands and cleaning windows.

"I'll buy the supper tonight, Aunty!" called Sam happily as he dashed out to Patel's, the corner shop.

He wandered round with a wire basket, trying to decide what to buy. The frozen food in the big fridge was much too expensive. He turned to the tins. He could buy say, one small tin of baked beans and one of rice pudding. He knew his Aunt was very partial to rice pudding ... But it didn't seem enough somehow.

Lost in thought Sam didn't see the display of cake-mixes piled up in a pyramid. He knocked into it sending packets and tins flying everywhere.

"Oh, SAM!" sighed Mrs Patel. "Do look where you're going! Now what is it you want, dear? You've been here ages!"

While Sam was on his hands and knees picking up the packets and tins he spotted a box in a corner of the shop. It was filled with tins, all without labels on.

"TEN PENCE EACH" said the notice.

"Please, what's in those tins?" asked Sam.

"Oh! That's our Lucky Dip," said Mrs Patel. "They've all lost their labels and we don't know what's in them. So you could get a nice tin of corned beef for only ten pence . . . But whatever's in them, they're a BAR-GAIN at that price!"

And Sam agreed. He could buy five tins for his fifty pence!

After some deliberation, he chose five, all different sizes and shapes.

That evening Uncle Dennis, Aunty
Kathleen and Sam sat down to a most
unusual supper of tomato soup, beet-
root and pineapple chunks.

Sam helped his Aunt clear the table.

"No one else has any odd jobs for me," he said. "What can I do?"

When they had finished putting the supper things away Sam and his Aunt sat down for a chat.

"What did *you* do, Aunty, if you needed to earn a bit of money, when you were a little girl?"

Aunty Kathleen smiled.

"It was all so different when I was a girl," she said. "First of all we weren't living in a block of flats in a city like this . . . we lived in a small country town. Let me think, what did we do? There were six of us children, and we were always hard up. I remember we used to take back empty bottles to the shop. Tuppence a bottle, I think we got. We used to collect them from all the neighbours . . . "

Aunty Kathleen went on. Although he liked to hear the stories of when she was a girl, Sam knew that nothing his Aunt did then would help him solve his problem now. Sam felt very miserable when he went to bed that night.

Chapter Three

On Saturday Sam went out on an errand. Uncle Dennis wanted a book called *How to Play Chess* from the library.

As Sam hurried along he felt something falling on his face: it was snowing! He stopped and gazed upwards, watching the snowflakes whirling down. The High Street was

busy with Christmas shoppers and
they bumped into him carrying
bulging bags of presents. He passed
the big store, Evans', and saw over
the main entrance a sign saying,
"ONLY SIXTEEN
MORE SHOPPING DAYS TO
CHRISTMAS".

When Sam arrived at the library, he was covered in snow. He got a bit lost inside. A lady librarian had to help him.

"You want the '*How to*' series," she said. She pointed out a row of red books on a shelf. Sam began to read the titles.

"*How to Play Golf. How to Write a Book. How to Speak Chinese . . .*"

And then he read a title that made his eyes grow round with excitement: "*How to Make a Fortune!*"

Sam seized it.

"At last! Now perhaps I'll get somewhere!" He took the book to be checked out. And there behind the counter was his old friend Bill, in his wheelchair. (Bill lived in Sam's block of flats on the ground floor.)

"Hello, Sam!" he said.

"Hello, Bill! I didn't know you worked here!" said Sam.

"Only odd days now and then," said Bill. When he saw the title of the book Sam had borrowed he threw back his head and roared with laughter.

"So you want to make a fortune, eh?" he chuckled.

Sam was a bit embarrassed. He didn't like Bill laughing like that.

"Well, my Aunty's lost her job, you see. And there's no money for Christmas," muttered Sam. "It's difficult to earn anything when you're a child. I only want to be useful . . ."

Bill stopped laughing and looked serious.

"Yes, I think I know how you feel, Sam," he said. "Look, the library shuts soon. Would you walk home with me, Sam? I'd like to hear your troubles . . ."

So Sam pushed Bill's wheelchair home. It was difficult because the snow was settling on the ground.

They paused outside the toy shop in the High Street.

"Lovely window, isn't it, Sam? Just look at that teddy-bear. It's as big as you!"

Sam pointed out the wooden castle. "Don't you think it's the best castle

you've ever seen, Bill?" Sam said, his eyes shining.

"At fifty pounds it jolly well ought to be!" said Bill.

Sam went into Bill's cosy flat for a cup of tea. And he told Bill all about his efforts to help his Aunt and Uncle. How he'd earned money doing odd jobs and bought tins of food.

"But I can't seem to earn very much. A few pence here and there doesn't really help. And I so wanted to buy Aunty the blue cardigan. Is there anything you can think of?" sighed Sam.

Bill stirred his cup of tea thoughtfully.

"Let's look at that book you got out of the library," he said, picking up *How to Make a Fortune*.

Bill studied it, frowning.

"'Investments, Banks, Stocks and Shares' . . . " He groaned and put the book down. "I'm afraid this isn't going to be any help, Sam."

65

Bill's wife Doris came in with some hot mince pies and they munched in silence for a while.

Then Bill smiled.

"Don't give up, Sam! Listen, I'm seeing someone about a job. I can't tell you much about it at the moment, but if I get this job — and it's a very

big IF — then you can be my helper, and earn some money. I'll know on Monday, so keep your fingers crossed, Sam!"

Sam went up in the lift to his home on the fifth floor.

A job! As Bill's helper! What could he possibly have in mind?

Uncle Dennis opened the door.

"Ah! My book! Thank you, Sam!"

He took it and settled down to read.

But when he put on his glasses and saw the title, *How to Make a Fortune*, he put it down again.

"Oh, Sam!" he sighed. "This is nothing to do with chess! How did you manage to get the wrong book?"

Chapter Four

Monday tea-time Sam went down to Bill's. Doris opened the door with a big smile.

"Come in, Sam, Bill's got some news for you!"

"I've got the job!" Bill cried excitedly. "Mind you, I must say it wasn't easy! I had to pass an audition first!"

68

"What's an audition?" said Sam, a bit puzzled.

"It's like a test for a job as an actor or musician," Bill explained. "To see if you fit the part . . . And I'd practised my Ho-ho-ho's all right! The job lasts for the next two weeks. Can you guess what it is now, Sam?"

Sam was more puzzled than ever.

"It's being Father Christmas at Evans'. You know, that big department store in the High Street. And you're to be Santa's Little Helper! What do you think, Sam? You'd earn fifty pounds, to be paid on Christmas Eve!"

Sam was speechless with delight. He'd be able to buy Christmas presents for his family now, all right!

"They've got a green elf suit for you to wear. And a ginger beard! What a laugh we'll have together, Sam!"

They were to start work the very next day in Santa's Grotto. Luckily for Sam, school had closed two weeks early as the central heating had broken down.

Sam tried on the green elf suit and it fitted him perfectly. And he liked wearing the big ginger beard so much he never wanted to take it off. He even wore it in the bath!

Bill made a wonderful Father Christmas. He would sit the children on his knee and ask in a deep, Santa voice what they wanted for Christmas. Then it was the elf's job to give the children their gifts, from the big sacks.

SANTAS GROTTO

TOYS

Sam loved his job. It was fun to be disguised. Even children from his school who came to the grotto didn't recognise him behind the big ginger beard!

The two weeks went by in a flash and soon it was Christmas Eve. Sam had earned FIFTY POUNDS! And he had all afternoon to do his shopping.

He and Bill set off together.

"This is great fun, Bill!" said Sam, his eyes shining. They bowled along the High Street at a brisk pace. Soon they were passing the wonderful toy shop.

"Shall we have a quick look . . . ?" said Sam.

As they looked in the window, a big
car drew up and a lady in a white fur
coat and a man got out. They hurried
into the shop and Sam saw the castle
being taken out of the window and
put in a big box. As they came out
carrying it Sam heard the lady say,
"That's just the thing for James!"

Sam felt a deep pang of disappointment . . .

"Right!" said Bill. "Let's do our shopping now!"

Sam bought: a beautiful blue cardigan for Aunty Kathleen; a chess set for Uncle Dennis; a Christmas cake with a little sugar robin on top; and as he still had some money over, he bought a present for Bill. It was a little Father Christmas in a round glass dome lined with snowflakes, and when you shook it made a lovely whirling snow-storm.

"Thank you, Sam! I've always wanted one of those!" chuckled Bill.

Sam couldn't wait to give his Aunty and Uncle their presents.

"It's a beautiful blue!" said Aunty Kathleen, slipping on the cardigan.

"And I love my chess set!" said Uncle Dennis. "We're both very proud of you, Sam!"

Then they all had tea with the Christmas cake with the little sugar robin on top.

On Christmas morning when Sam woke up he could tell at once that everything was all right: there was the smell of eggs and bacon cooking, the fire was on, and he could hear Christmas carols coming from the radio.

Sam pulled on his dressing-gown, eager for his breakfast. He couldn't help wondering if there might be a

little present for him after all. Sam
dashed into the other room and
stopped in amazement. He couldn't
believe his eyes! There on the floor
was a huge CASTLE!

And it was even bigger and better than the one in the toy shop! Not only did it have battlements and towers, but a real little drawbridge you could raise up and down, and a flag flying from the tallest tower. It was a truly magnificent castle.

"HAPPY CHRISTMAS, SAM!" cried Aunty Kathleen. "While you were away being Santa's little helper, your Uncle worked day and night to make it . . . "

"Do you like it, Sam?" said Uncle Dennis.

"Like it? It's the best castle EVER," he said. "And you can't buy one like it in any toy shop in the world! But how did you know I wanted a castle, Uncle?" said Sam, as he arranged his best knights along the battlements.

"Ah ha!" said his Uncle. "Father Christmas told me!"

THE GHOST AT NO. 13
Gyles Brandreth

Hamlet Brown's sister, Susan, is just too perfect. Everything she does is praised and Hamlet is in despair – until a ghost comes to stay for a holiday and helps him to find an exciting idea for his school project!

RADIO DETECTIVE
John Escott

A piece of amazing deduction by the Roundbay Radio Detective when Donald, the radio's young presenter, solves a mystery but finds out more than anyone expects.

RAGDOLLY ANNA'S CIRCUS
Jean Kenward

Made only from a morsel of this and a tatter of that, Ragdolly Anna is a very special doll and the six stories in this book are all about her adventures.

SEE YOU AT THE MATCH
Margaret Joy

Six delightful stories about football. Whether spectator, player, winner or loser these short, easy stories for young readers are a must for all football fans.

ONE NIL

Tony Bradman

Dave Brown is mad about football and when he learns that the England squad are to train at the local City ground he thinks up a brilliant plan to overcome his parents' objections and get him to the ground to see them.

ON THE NIGHT WATCH

Hannah Cole

A group of children and their parents occupy their tiny school in an effort to prevent its closure.

FIONA FINDS HER TONGUE

Diana Hendry

At home Fiona is a chatterbox but whenever she goes out she just won't say a word. How she overcomes her shyness and 'finds her tongue' is told in this charming book.

IT'S TOO FRIGHTENING FOR ME!

Shirley Hughes

The eerie old house gives Jim and Arthur the creeps. But somehow they just can't resist poking around it, even when a mysterious white face appears at the window! A deliciously scary story – for brave readers only!

THE CONKER AS HARD AS A DIAMOND

Chris Powling

Last conker season Little Alpesh had lost every single game! But this year it's going to be different and he's going to be Conker Champion of the Universe! The trouble is, only a conker as hard as a diamond will make it possible – and where on earth is he going to find one?

JOSH'S PANTHER

Fay Sampson

Josh never meant to deceive anyone about the paw print but his sister was such a clever know-all he just couldn't let her crow over him yet again.

RED LETTER DAY

Alexa Romanes

It was meant to be such a very special day in the village but it did seem at one time as if the whole thing would end in disaster . . .

SUN AND RAIN

Ann Ruffell

The heatwave seemed to go on for ever, but with the help of a rain-making kit Susan managed to produce a solitary rain cloud.

THE RELUCTANT DRAGON

Kenneth Grahame

The Boy was not at all surprised to find a Dragon on the South Downs, but he was surprised to find that it was so civilized.

MR MAJEIKA AND THE HAUNTED HOTEL

Humphrey Carpenter

Life is never dull for Class Three of St Barty's School. With a teacher like Mr Majeika, who is also a magician, anything can happen – and usually does.